Faber has published children's books since 1929. T. S. Eliot's *Old Possum's Book of Practical Cats* and Ted Hughes' *The Iron Man* were amongst the first. Our catalogue at the time said that 'it is by reading such books that children learn the difference between the shoddy and the genuine'. We still believe in the power of reading to transform children's lives. All our books are chosen with the express intention of growing a love of reading, a thirst for knowledge and to cultivate empathy. We pride ourselves on responsible editing. Last but not least, we believe in kind and inclusive books in which all children feel represented and important.

For my Vent group, Circle, and the Swaggers × R.S.

For Lex, stay free R.P.

First published in the UK in 2022
First published in the US in 2022
by Faber and Faber Limited
Bloomsbury House,
74–77 Great Russell Street,
London WC1B 3DA
faberchildrens.co.uk
Text © Rashmi Sirdeshpande 2022
Illustrations © Rikin Parekh 2022
Designed by Faber and Faber

US HB ISBN 978–0–571–37476–2
PB ISBN 978–0–571–35966–0

MIX
Paper from
responsible sources
FSC
www.fsc.org
FSC® C016779

The moral rights of Rashmi Sirdeshpande and Rikin Parekh have been asserted.

A CIP record for this book is available from the British Library.

This is Cow.

Cow is the Next **Big Thing.**

Cow, say hello.

And this is Moon.
And Cat.
And Dog.
And Dish.
And Spoon.

You know how this goes, don't you?

Hey diddle diddle, the cat and the fiddle,
The cow jumped over . . .

Has anyone seen Cow?

Cow, what ARE you doing?

MOOoo!

You're hiding? What on earth for?
Come back here this instant!
You're holding everyone up.

Right, that's better. Let's try that again.
With the cow this time. **FROM THE TOP . . .**

Hey diddle diddle, the cat and the fiddle,
The cow jumped over . . .
COW! This is your bit.

Cow, what do you mean you can't do it?

MOOoo

No, we can't just cut that bit out. It's the main part of the story!

Right. I've had enough of this. You think I can't find another cow who'd love this job?

Why, I can think of a hundred cows who'd jump at the chance to star in *Hey Diddle Diddle*.

Okay, OKAY, you're right. I was too harsh . . .
Cat, put the fiddle down and get Cow some tissues.

Okay, Cow. I'm sorry I yelled at you.
I get it. You're scared. You don't think you
can jump over the moon.

Now, tell us –
what exactly are you afraid will happen?

You can't be worried about people laughing at you, Cow.

"The little dog laughed to see such FUN", remember? He's not laughing at YOU.
No one's going to laugh at YOU!

Well, okay, they might.
But that's okay!

Look, I have an idea . . .

Why don't you start small?
Start with ONE brave thing?
Like jumping over Dish.

Oh, don't look at me like that.
You can't do it . . . YET.
Now, come on . . .

YOU DID IT, Cow! By George, YOU DID IT!

Now let's try Dog . . .

DOG? Where are you? Oh, for goodness' sake.

Cat, then. You can jump over Cat and the fiddle.
Yes you CAN, Cow.
We BELIEVE in you. Don't we, chaps?

Right.

READY . . . STEADY . . . GO!

You DID it, Cow! YOU DID IT!
Now for the biggie . . . **Moon?**

Can someone lower
Moon down a notch?

Lovely. Off you go, Cow.

Yes you can, Cow! We believe in you!

READY . . .

STEADY . . .

GO . . .

MOOoo

Yes *you can*, Cow.
Things don't always work out the first time.

Sometimes, the best thing to do is to dust yourself off and **do it again.**

Oh Cow, please don't go . . .

You FAILED? Why, that's WONDERFUL! CONGRATULATIONS!

The worst that can happen has already happened.

The hardest bit is out of the way! But look – if you still want to go, that's quite alright, Cow.

The main thing is that you did your best . . .

YOU DID IT, COW!

YOU DID IT!

We KNEW you could. You're READY.
And just in time! Phew!

Come along Cat, Dog, Dish and Spoon.
You too, Moon. The audience is waiting!

Hey diddle diddle, the cat and the fiddle,
The cow jumped OVER the moon!
The little dog laughed to see such fun
And the dish ran away with the spoon!

The End